Kuchisake-Onna

口裂け女

K.N. Nguyen

www.dragonscript.net

Cover design by Brian Flores and Francis Nguyen.

Layouts by Francis Nguyen.

ISBN-13 978-1-949322-20-0

Thank you, Alicia

Your help has been invaluable

I'll see you at taiko

I

Minamoto Chō wandered through the busy streets of Tokyo. Bodies flowed around her like a stream parting around rocks. Sunlight danced across the strands of her jet-black hair that framed her shoulders. If anyone paid attention, they would've marveled at how perfect it was. It was more beautiful than a polished piece of obsidian; her pride and joy. A pale pink bow with plastic strawberries sat clipped above her ear, the soft color drawing attention to the faint glow that tinged her cheeks. The light turned green and Chō joined the sea of people rushing to cross the street. Countless bodies pressed forward, many talking on cellular phones, weaving between their neighbors in an effort to reach the other side. And ultimately, their final destination.

All but Chō. She moved without any urgency. She would arrive when she needed to. There was no reason to rush through life, no reason to stress the serenity of her soul. Life moved in an eternal cycle, and she planned to enjoy the ride.

A man in a freshly pressed suit nearly bumped into Chō as he hurried past while talking on his phone. She stutter-stepped to the left just in time, the edge of his briefcase slicing the air where she had just been. Before she could regain her footing, a car roared past, its wake whipping at her skirts. The man didn't slow, didn't glance back, too busy to notice the near collision she'd barely avoided.

Chō glared at the man's retreating form. *Everyone is in too much of a hurry.* Sticking her tongue out at the now vanished man, Chō continued on.

She found herself turning down several streets, the giant buildings a monolith casting shadows onto the ground and cooling the otherwise warm day quite nicely. Not more than fifteen minutes later, she found herself standing outside a popular toy store. Through the windows, she watched small children pull their parents from one shiny toy to the next. The sparkle in their eyes as they spied something new brought a warm feeling to Chō's stomach.

Not having anything pressing to do for the next hour, Chō decided to indulge herself and walked inside. The artificial lights were blinding compared to the pleasant gloom outside. Chō's eyes, a rich, dark brown, began to water behind her thick lashes. Blinking several times, a wave of relief washed over Chō as her eyes finally adjusted to the brightness. Taking a look around, Chō noticed how the toys almost glowed under the bright lights. Brilliantly colored miniatures called out to her, begging to be held and played with. Further in, she saw a large display of stuffed animals. The mountain of white ducks in blue shirts, yellow dogs, cute mice – some with large polka dot bows – and tan bears sat arranged in the center of one of the store's rooms.

A smile filled Chō's face as she picked up one of the tan teddy bears. A pale, almost white fur framed its face. The little bear wore a sailor suit and matching hat, much like the duck. She held the bear while examining the plush mountain. On the wall opposite the stuffed animals, Chō spied the bear clutched in her hands in keychain form. Returning the plushie, she picked up the keychain and continued on through the large store.

Countless trinkets were arranged to catch her attention. Cute cropped shirts with characters or fun phrases hung off the walls. More miniatures lay stacked in another corner. All around her, décor and wall paintings added to the whimsical ambiance in the store. Near the register, Chō found herself drawn to a glass case. Inside she found what called to her.

A pair of cherry blossom earrings caught her attention, the delicate blossoms dangled from dainty gold chains. The cute earrings and matching hairpin stared back at her. The two were so elegant that they almost seemed out of place amongst mouse-shaped jewelry in the rest of the case. The light in this section of the store was especially bright, causing the stones and gold to shine under the glass. The delicate accessories begged to be taken home. Her breath caught in her throat. She had to have them.

Just then, an employee walked over with a teenaged girl. The employee opened the case and took out a simple silver necklace with a silver bow to take with them to the register. Chō grabbed the cherry blossom earrings and hairpin before the employee locked the case once more. She continued to wander through the store, taking in the joy and excitement of the children around her. A few glanced at Chō then quickly turned away as some new bauble caught their attention. After her encounter with the man in the suit, it was nice not to feel invisible.

A gentle tinkling from a nearby phone startled Chō as she admired a display of hair ribbons. The little rainbow of silk and fabric quickly faded from the corner of her eye as a spike of panic surged through her. It was almost ten. Her heart skipped a beat as the uncharacteristic worry from being late caused her to nearly drop the trinkets she held. Without thinking, she turned and hurried out of the store. It wasn't until several blocks later that she remembered the bear keychain, earrings, and hairpin still clutched in her hand.

I guess I can't go back there again, Chō thought nonchalantly as she wove the cherry blossom hairpin into her hair. She removed the pink bow, the clip striking her head as she opened it. The dainty pin suited her much better.

Popping in the earrings, Chō continued on her way. She had an early lunch date and couldn't be late. There was no use concerning herself with trivial things like accidental shoplifting.

Pressing forward with a speedy gait, Chō continued on until a little café located on a side street came into view. A quaint little place with a few circular tables out front, Chō could smell the freshly baked pastries that tempted her from the glass display case inside. There were already a few people seated outside with cups of coffee or tea. Grabbing a table, Chō waited for her date to arrive. She had met Shō on the train a few weeks ago. He'd been reading when she caught his eye - a college student from the local university.

Over time, they got closer. His voice both soft and melodic, lulled her into a trance every time they met, and his laugh made her melt. Chō found herself finding excuses to take the same train just so she could see him. He usually traveled with his friends, the group breaking the common etiquette on the train of keeping silent and sharing small, stilted conversations. Chō sat demurely beside them, batting her thick lashes every time she caught his gaze.

It had been Shō who recommended meeting at this café. His personality was more forward than most of the boys Chō met, and that confident and outgoing exterior appealed to her. Chō liked strong men.

Picking up a cup of green tea, Chō played nervously with the teddy bear keychain. The texture was oddly relaxing. Its fuzzy body soothed her as she ran her fingers over the fur. Minutes dragged by. Her tea slowly became cold. Then, she spotted him.

Dressed in a white t-shirt and khaki pants, Shō made Chō's breath catch in her throat and her heart race. He called out an apology for being late as he readjusted the strap of his backpack handing off his shoulder.

He's so polite. Chō blushed as he approached. Glancing at her reflection in the café window, she noticed the pink of her cheeks accentuating her elegant cheekbones and giving the tip of her nose a doll-like appearance. With a coy smile, she tucked a strand of hair behind her ear, dropping her head ever so slightly and staring at him through her lashes.

Walking over to Shō with her head kept down demurely, she replied, "No need to apologize. I lost track of time as well."

"I hope you haven't been waiting long." His voice was rich like honey.

Chō melted.

"It's all right."

That voice wasn't hers.

Chō's voice caught in her throat as Shō wrapped his arms around another girl with light brown hair that walked up from behind her. The two shared a quick kiss before Shō slipped his arm around the girl's waist and led her into the café. Chō's heart fell into the pit that suddenly appeared in her stomach. Her eyes burned. Lightly touching her cheek, Chō felt a thin trail as another tear rolled down her face.

"Why?" she whispered as the young couple ordered drinks and a snack. "Why?"

Her cup forgotten on the table, Chō turned and staggered away. This was their date. He was supposed to be having lunch with her. He promised.

Why would Shō do that?

Chō moved through the city, her feet following familiar paths while the buildings and streets blurred around her, barely registering the world passing by. She hadn't been embarrassed like this in such a long time.

After some unknown period of time - Chō couldn't even guess at the time – she found herself in a small park. A river flowed through the verdant lawn, the Ginkgo and Sakura trees providing a picturesque canopy to shade the lovers who walked down the path. Off in the distance, she saw a few older ladies sitting at a picnic table, their silver hair shining in the sun. Swiping away the tear that rolled down her cheek, Chō sat down and took off her shoes. The lush grass felt nice under her porcelain feet. Leaving her shoes under a Sakura tree, Chō walked barefoot through the park, allowing the gentle breeze to play with her hair and the sweet smell of the pale pink cherry blossoms to take away her embarrassment.

II

A pair of women laughed, their botefuri swaying side-to-side as they made their way to the market to sell fish and onigiri. The small wooden baskets dangling from the ropes didn't appear to bother them. The sun beat down on their muscular backs, a slight tan darkening their otherwise perfect skin. Chō watched as the two women, clearly farmer's wives or some kind of peasant, carried on without a car in the world. Her lip curled up in a sneer as she tracked the two women meandering down the dirt road opposite to the field she traversed. Her chest swelled with pride. She didn't have to struggle or perform menial labor just to survive. She was blessed with being born into the proper social class and been able to make the right connections.

The tall grasses tickled Chō's feet as she walked barefoot through the wide field. The silks of her many-layered jūnihitoe rustled with each step. Rich raspberry reds accented with layers of white, gold, and green completed the ensemble. A gold crescent moon hairpin pinning her obsidian hair into an elegant, twisting bun added a dramatic touch. In the distance, the lowing of cattle punctuated the birdsong as other farmers harvested their rice.

Her mobakama lay forgotten at home in her hinoki wood armoire, the simple skirt a symbol of her constrictions. Though it wasn't as physically constricting, Chō hated the way it choked her into purity and submission. A beautiful woman like her deserved to be free to enjoy life the way she wanted – a goddess among the simple folk – and her clothes reflected her desire to be seen and admired.

Pink cosmos flowers dotted the luscious green grass, their light fragrance tickling her button nose. A chill breeze kicked up, bringing gooseflesh to her porcelain skin. Chō tugged at the outermost layer of her uwagi despite knowing the silk robe would not make her any warmer. Luckily, Tatsuzō would keep her plenty warm.

Maple trees marked the perimeter of the field. Behind her, Chō knew that the cherry blossom trees would obscure her travel through the open field enough that by the time she reached the maples no one would see her. Tatsuzō was younger than her, and if anyone saw them together it would become quite the scandal and people would talk more than they already did. The middle son of a local farmer, his strong hands and lean body belied his baby face.

Tatsuzō waited under the shade of a maple, his deep blue kimono stood out to Chō against the delicate kaleidoscope of greens, pinks, and pale browns of nature. It was almost the same velvety color of night, and in the shadows, it helped conceal him from those who only spared a glance. A smile broke out on his face and he stepped out to meet her, pulling her back into the privacy of the trees as he kissed her full lips. Affection rained down onto her neck with no preamble – Tatsuzō's mouth hungry for her own, and her flesh.

A giggle escaped Chō's red-painted lips, but she didn't move to push him away. Her mouth met his and they shared a passionate kiss. Chō's body melted into Tatsuzō's. His hands tightly gripped her slender waist, pulling her closer into him. The couple stood together sharing fervent kisses for several long minutes. Wanting more, Chō broke away and looked deeply into his eyes, biting her bottom lip as her hand trailed along his chest. She felt his breath hitch and his body press against hers. Lightly taking his hand with hers, Chō led him to their secret spot, shooting occasional smiles over her shoulder, drawing him in further.

Underneath a collection of willow trees, a well-worn indent in the grass indicated the lover's rendezvous location. Chō dipped down onto the lush grass and shrugged off her outer robe, revealing a tempting flash of skin. Pulling the hairpin free, Chō's raven hair cascaded down around her shoulders. Tatsuzō took her in hungrily. She could see the lust in his eyes. Batting her thick eyelashes, Chō glanced up at him demurely.

He quickly joined her on the ground and rained kisses all over her once more. His lips roved over her body – peppering them greedily onto her mouth before tenderly brushing them down her neck until she reached the hollow of her throat. One hand pulled at the collar of her jūnihitoe, briefly getting caught in one of the many layers before exposing more flesh. His other hand traveled up her thigh and underneath her skirts.

Chō's hand reached behind Tatsuzō's head, bringing him closer. Her other hand worked to undo his kimono. The familiar feeling of anticipation shot through her as his fingers found what they searched for. Her mouth pressed roughly against his as he continued to rub his fingers over her. Her body became hot as Tatsuzō's fingers moved inside her. Not wanting to wait much longer, Chō threw off his kimono. Tatsuzō's lean body didn't have much muscle, but he was still strong. In one swift motion, he pulled Chō onto his lap until she straddled him.

By this point, Chō's clothes had been discarded and were sitting in a pile nearby. The two shared fevered kisses, their bodies entangled on the bent grass. Their hands traveled over each other, exploring each spot that brought a little moan from their lips. Tatsuzō's fingers pumped quickly, each one bringing him to that sweet spot inside Chō and sending a thrill through her. Chō wanted to push his head down, but she couldn't bring herself to stop him. Finally, Tatsuzō climbed on top of her. Chō's breathing came out in ecstatic gasps, her breathy moans becoming louder as Tatsuzō's own joined hers.

Their stolen time passed by in a blur of passionate kisses and a tangle of arms and legs. Tatsuzō's body moved with her own, each thrust becoming harder and faster as her body clenched around him. Sweat beaded on their flesh and blended together, their kisses becoming sloppy with each gasp of pleasure. In a moment of euphoric bliss, the two shared one last, long kiss before Tatsuzō rolled off of Chō. Their chests rose and fell rapidly as they struggled for breath between smaller kisses.

Each visit with Tatsuzō was better than the last.

"When can I see you again?" he asked.

"I'm not sure," Chō replied. "My husband is returning soon." Taking a moment, Chō tried to calculate when they could meet up again. "By the full moon."

Two weeks.

Two weeks until she could feel his body again.

Tatsuzō gently grabbed Chō's chin and brought her in for another kiss. "Can't you come out after he's asleep?"

Chō shook her head. "I have to be there for Sakanoue-sama. Ietsuna-dono and his regents are giving him a break after chasing the rōnin. He's going to want to spend some time with me."

Tatsuzō grumbled a few choice curses and gnashed his teeth.

Leaning over, he parted Chō's legs and brough his lips to her left inner thigh. She wished his tongue were elsewhere, but a small shiver coursed through her as he left a mark on her soft flesh.

"Until the full moon," he said as his head popped up.

"Until the full moon," she purred.

By the time Chō found herself crossing the empty field, the sun hung low in the horizon, ready to set. She worked to smooth her silks as she walked, not bothering to pin up her hair once again. The last month had been fun. Tatsuzō proved to be her best lover yet. She wondered how long it would last before she became bored with him. The seventeen-year-old left her feeling young and desirable.

No use worrying. She would stay with him until she tired of his company.

The sun started creeping below the horizon as Chō walked onto her estate. The well-tended lawn parted as a simple dirt trail led up to her home. A cherry blossom tree stood in the yard, a wooden bench resting underneath for her husband to sit on while he read. Picturing Sakanoue Shōtarō on the bench, his brow furrowed in concentration as he read, brought a smile to her lips. Shōtarō's statuesque features were a blessing from the gods. The image didn't fade as the seconds passed on. It was almost as though a phantom of her husband sat quietly. Chō found herself enjoying the moment despite being wrapped in the arms of another only minutes before.

"Milady!" a high-pitched voice called out from somewhere near Chō's home.

Chō turned from the bench where the image of Shōtarō still rested. She watched as one of her servants raced down the steps towards her. Chō raised a brow. Curiosity got the better of her.

The girl covered the distance between the two in the span of a few heartbeats. Her geta slapped the ground in a frantic rhythm, giving the spritely girl's steps a noticeable *thump* as she ran.

"Milady," she gasped as she stood in front of Chō. "I have bad news."

"What is it?" Chō hissed.

The girl was supposed to keep the rest of the house staff from knowing that she'd gone out for the afternoon.

The young servant's brow was beaded with sweat and a faint pink flush from her dash tinged her delicate cheeks. Despite it all, her beauty displeased Chō as she quickly forgot the announcement of bad news. As the woman of the house, Chō should be the most stunning at all times. Heads turned when Chō walked through the village. If word got out that a mere servant rivaled her mistress' beauty – well, she may have to remedy that. But for now...

"Sakanoue-sama has returned home early, Milady. He's been asking for you."

Chō's stomach dropped. Her hands flew to her head and hastily tried to smooth the hair of her now messy bun. She hoped the paint on her lips hadn't smudged too much. Chō remembered seeing a faint red tint on Tatsuzō's lips before they went their separate ways.

"I've been looking for you," a rich tenor called out. Though he didn't yell, Shōtarō's voice carried over the yard clearly and hit Chō like a punch in the stomach.

III

Flickering yellow light from the street lamps and the occasional headlight broke the blackness. Stores were closed and despite it not being too late, no one appeared to be in a rush to get to their final destination. Clouds blocked the moon and muted the stars. Chō's surroundings mirrored her soul – dark and empty. Why had Shō misled her like that? A singular tear rolled down her cheek.

Not wanting to be seen crying, Chō placed a face mask over her mouth and nose to hide any discoloration from her ruddy cheeks and smudges caused by her red eyeliner. Her eyes were hot after an afternoon of sobbing. At least her nose finally stopped running. She hated not looking perfect, and this vulnerability left her feeling ugly both inside and out.

Chō briefly wondered why she cared so much about her appearance. It seemed she worried about it more than most girls her age. Somewhere deep down, the indescribable feeling of being lost tickled the back of her mind and constricted her breathing. Chō tried to concentrate on the sensation, but couldn't bring it any further into focus. Lost and alone – the two emotions lay hidden so far in her mind. Chō couldn't figure out why, but they felt like she experienced them a lifetime ago. One long forgotten.

No one passed Chō as she struggled to compose herself. Still, she kept the mask on. She couldn't risk it. With each step, the heaviness that settled over her began simmering until it bubbled over into an overwhelming desire to smash something.

He will pay, she seethed. *No one embarrasses me.*

Her knuckles turned white from her clenched fist. Her nails bit into her palms, creating little crescent moons in her flesh. All the disrespect she'd experienced that day boiled within her, looking for an outlet for release. Blocks passed by in a red haze and gradually the volatile emotions inside simmered down, leaving Chō to wander the darkened streets in a state of apathy. The absence of emotion drained her.

A cool night breeze caressed her face, serving as a balm to soothe her frayed nerves as it played with loose strands of her hair. Chō closed her eyes and stopped for a moment. She stood still for a few heartbeats, taking deep breaths to wash away the last remnants of the chaos that swirled inside and leaving her hollow, but at peace. The soft winds reminded her of a light spring shower, one that washed away all cares and leaving her pure yet again.

Chō began to wonder if she overreacted. Perhaps she had misunderstood Shō's words.

"Excuse me."

A soft voice, that of a child, brought Chō back to reality. Standing before her, Chō saw a little girl no more than eight. The girl wore a backpack and school uniform. Her clear eyes watched Chō with the subtle apprehension that a child afraid of the dark tries to hide behind a façade of big kid bravado. However, Chō noticed how the girl shifted from foot to foot.

Blinking heavily, Chō realized she stood in the middle of the sidewalk, blocking the girl's line of travel. The only other way past was by walking into the traffic that picked up as after-school classes and shift work ended.

"Excuse me," the young girl said again. There was a note of urgency to her tone this time – and a slight quiver that must have slipped out while she attempted to politely get Chō's attention.

All of the day's events came tumbling out in one moment. A tidal wave of anger, embarrassment, and self-pity hit her full force, threatening to bring forth a wall of tears once again despite her efforts to banish them. The girl must have noticed Chō's anguish because the concern on her face disappeared, replaced with the sweet, innocent, sympathy that young children share with their friends.

"Am I pretty?" Chō asked.

God, why does it matter?

She thought of Shō and the cute girl sitting together at the café, holding hands as they sipped their drinks. Chō wanted to feel the warmth of his arm around her waist and his lips against hers just as she had imagined for the last several weeks. In her mind, his touch would be tender, yet passionate. Her body craved this closeness.

"Y-yes?" the girl stammered, confused by the question.

A flood of relief filled Chō like water poured into a cup. The sensation spilled over, pushing out the emotions that loomed in the back of her mind. Children were honest. Small wrinkles around the corners of Chō's eyes formed as she smiled, the edge of her mask crinkling up.

The mask.

Chō forgot to remove it as she wandered the streets in her haze of negativity. Slipping it off, Chō faced the girl once more.

"What about now?" she asked.

Chō had her answer, but the tiny spark of vanity that twinkled in her soul demanding to be fed. Like the flame of a candle, it hungered for more.

The girl hesitated, glancing at the street before mumbling a response. Her lack of a direct answer frustrated Chō. Why couldn't people communicate properly? The girl had just given her an honest answer moments before. Chō knew she wasn't ugly, but her ego needed to be appeased. Taking a step towards the girl, Chō's world went black.

IV

A dull ache behind Chō's eyes woke her up. With a groan, she rubbed her head. As soon as her palm touched her temple, she recoiled. The pain spiked at her touch.

"What happened?" she mumbled. Her hoarse voice cracked. "Water."

Moving gingerly so as not to anger her head, Chō pushed herself to her feet. Her hair hung limply around her face, its normal gloss and neat appearance ruined. Even her clothes were disheveled – wrinkles and stains marred her usually pristine outfit.

Her apartment was dark, the only light coming from the sunlight that bled through the blinds. Her shoes lay strewn in the hallway instead of resting in their normal spot by the front door. Stumbling through her small home, Chō made her way to the kitchen for a glass of water. As she sipped from her favorite mug, Chō noticed a faint glint on the floor.

Chō crouched, her fingers brushing against something smooth and cool. Her cherry blossom hairpin lay on the floor, its delicate petals smeared with something dark. She turned it between her fingers, her stomach tightening as she noticed the same stains streaking her skin. A sharp breath hitched in her throat. The pin slipped from her grasp, so did the mug in her other hand. The crash of ceramic against the floor sent jagged shards scattering across the room, but the sound barely registered. Chō's hands trembled as she turned them over, staring at the stains marring her pale skin. It almost looked like blood.

Her breath came out in ragged gasps and her body trembled.

"No," she whispered.

As quick as she dared, Chō ran to the bathroom. Blood stained her hands all the way up her arms. Splatter dotted her blouse as well. Turning on the faucet, Chō scrubbed at the blood on her flesh, muttering to herself. The hot water burned her skin, and she scrubbed so hard that she nearly tore the skin off her arms, but she couldn't stop until the last dregs of blood ran down the drain and swirled into oblivion. At last she was clean. Changing her clothes, Chō made her way back to the living area in a state of shock. The bloodied hairpin and broken mug remained forgotten on the floor.

The warm light of the television filled the room and a low monotone voice droned on. Chō sat in a chair, her mind in a daze. Her hand reached for the knitting needles on the small table in front of her, but her mind was a jumbled mess that she wanted to disentangle.

How did I get hurt? Was it on the way home? Did I get drunk?

Her mind reeled, but she didn't remember anything. Only Shō and his betrayal.

"Police are asking for help identifying a young girl found stabbed to death this morning," a cool female voice said. "Cameras in the area have not revealed any information."

Chō snapped out of her fog. In the glow of the television, she barely listened as the reporter motioned to the flurry of police movement. Something in the back of Chō's mind tingled. The location looked familiar.

"Police have not yet determined the time of death, but they believe it was late last night or sometime early this morning."

Oh no, Chō thought. *That must have happened after I left. Poor thing. That could have been me.*

Chō's breath caught in her throat at the thought of encountering the monster who was capable of brutally killing a child. It easily could have been her instead.

What if he was following me? What if he caught me and... and violated me?

She watched the report, her mind not quite paying attention to what was being said, before shutting off the television. Chō sat in her chair in a stupor, her mind numb. A nagging feeling wiggled its way into the back of her head and wouldn't let go. Try as she might, Chō couldn't shake free the thought that she had been at the location. Why else would she be covered in blood?

"Did I get attacked too?" she mused aloud. "It makes sense. Why else would my head hurt and my pin be covered in blood?"

As if on cue, Chō realized that the throbbing pain in her head had subsided. Humming in relief, the situation still brought questions of its own. Waking up in pain was not a good way to start the day. Her mind raced, but she didn't have the energy to try and piece everything together. No matter how hard she tried, she couldn't remember a thing. Sighing, Chō hoped that giving herself some time would bring answers to her questions. For now, she would move on.

Should I go to the police? she wondered. *What would I say?*

A knock on the door startled Chō.

"Anyone here?" a voice called through the door.

"Yes," Chō replied, struggling to her feet and shuffling over to the door.

With her hand on the knob, Chō overheard the building manager and a few other male voices talking about clearing the hallway.

"There's shattered glass everywhere," one said. "It's a miracle no one has cut themselves on it yet."

General chatter about how to proceed and how the glass got there to begin with continued. One of her neighbors stepped outside, asking the manager what happened. Turning from the door, Chō made her way back to her chair just as they started talking about one of the apartments being empty for a while and additional maintenance that needed to be done to the floor.

Let them handle the mess outside by themselves.

Did I fall? I don't see any cuts, but how else would I get so much blood on me?

Checking her body once more, Chō didn't find any big wounds on her arms or legs. This time, she noticed a few small scratches on her arms, but chalked them up to when she scrubbed her arms clean earlier that morning.

I must have hit my head trying to avoid the glass, Chō concluded. *Damn you, Shō!*

Not wanting to spiral again, Chō went to her room to change. Shō was a waste of time, and now her schedule opened up leaving the morning free for her to wander about. She thought about calling in sick to the maid café where she worked, but decided against it. Despite her best efforts at showcasing the simple elegance of her natural beauty, no one ever took a picture with her at the café. It was as though she were invisible to the rest of the world. Even when she dropped off parfaits and drinks, no one engaged with her – and if she didn't take enough pictures, she wouldn't be seen as a desirable waitress. It was a cruel numbers game every maid café played with their girls to keep them bubbly and making money for the business.

They're probably going to fire me anyway, she thought bitterly. *Unless I can get someone to notice me.*

Combing her long hair, Chō was pleased to see the luster return. A smile filled her face as her pride and joy returned to its expected beauty. For years, she'd been growing her hair, treating it with the best oils to help it shine. Once satisfied with its glow, Chō moved to apply her make up. She didn't need to look in a mirror – all she did was add a little pink to her cheeks and put on a smear of pale pink lipstick. Natural beauty was best.

Chō tied the pastel pink ribbon on the front of her blouse, pulling the edges tight to make a large bow. Admiring her outfit, Chō smoothed any wrinkles before heading out. Remembering the little keychain she left at the café, Chō decided to see if they still had it. She spied her hairpin among the mess on the floor. Picking it up, Chō washed off the blood and stuck it back into her hair.

V

Shōtarō's broad shoulders were bare, only his black hakama clothing him. A long, thin scar ran along his back, a reminder of a rogue's attack. Chō took in his lean figure, his muscles relaxed, yet still defined. Shōtarō did not acknowledge her presence. The lack of greeting sent a surge of anger through her. Not wanting him to see her reaction to his snub, Chō took a deep breath and plastered on a pleasant expression on her face. Hoping she did not appear harsh, Chō pressed forward.

Crossing the space between them, Chō traced her fingers down his spine. The tips of her fingers lightly caressed his flesh, causing the muscles to involuntarily twitch.

"You're home early, otto." Chō's voice dripped like poisoned honey. "You've been gone much too long. I missed you."

"I'm sure." Shōtarō did not move to face her, his words terse.

Chō bristled at the affront. Her words could melt the hardest exterior. Gently grabbing his arm and spinning him around until he faced her, Chō put on a saccharine tone, staring seductively at her husband. "Come now." Her fingers traced his jawline, lightly touching his lips before trailing down to his chest. "Surely, you don't mean that." Meeting his steely gaze, Chō bit her red lip and bat her lashes. "Come with me. I can help you relax."

Waiting expectantly, Chō resumed her caressing. A muscle spasmed in his jaw. Shōtarō refused to meet her gaze. Instead, he stared past her. Angered, Chō moved her hands lower. She was rewarded with a slight quiver from his abdominal region.

No one could resist her.

†

It was by a stroke of luck that Chō found her keychain at the café. A server found it the previous afternoon, storing it in the employee lounge in case someone claimed it. She found herself wishing that the wait staff would at least acknowledge her instead of making Chō go to the back to grab the keychain herself. Everyone seemed so preoccupied with their own lives.

Now, Chō wandered the streets. Try as she might, she couldn't get over the feeling of being invisible. People only seemed to respond to her when she was upset.

She'd made direct eye contact with Shō several times. There was no way he was talking to someone else. She even caught him breathing in her fragrance on the couple occasions they'd been pressed together while they held on to the hand rails. Each time, he was a perfect gentleman despite the way he gave her that boyish wink. Chō remembered even meeting some of his friends and having conversations about the difficulties they had with different instructors. Their time together was personal. Special. Yet, with each step, Chō swallowed her pride as she came to terms with the very real reality that she had been wrong.

Bastard, she thought, her eyes downcast in shame.

Chō couldn't even muster up the energy to cry. It was as though the very essence of her being had faded away. She was empty.

A shoulder roughly bumped into her, pulling her back from her reverie. By the time she spun around, a tall man on his phone was nearly at the end of the street. Chō glowered at the casually dressed man. There was no excuse for that kind of rudeness.

"What the hell?" Chō called out, her voice cracking as though she were about to cry.

The man ignored her. As his back disappeared into the distance, Chō found herself standing rooted to the spot, seething like a petulant child. No sooner did he vanish from her sight did she stomp her foot and scream in rage.

"Damn assholes!" she shrieked into the ether. "Why do they ignore me? I'm right here."

No heads turned to face her during her outburst. Everyone just continued on, oblivious to Chō and her anguish. Her tantrum continued as she slowly traveled down a side-street. Her shrill cries were punctuated with occasional curses at the world. People parted around her as though she were a rock in a swiftly moving river. Chō wished a vending machine would pop up so she could take her rage out on it. The urge to strike or kick something almost overwhelmed her. She needed an outlet for the swirling vortex that was her ire. Hours passed before the intensity of her emotion petered out, leaving her to trudge along in a daze.

I hate them all.

Bodies passed by, giving her a wide berth as she walked. At some point, Chō pulled on a face mask to hide her tear-streaked face. She hated how her nose became cherry red when she cried. If only she could hide her eyes.

I should just kill myself.

Her brooding turned dark as she struggled to find a reason to continue on. No, she would not give Shō – she would not give *anyone* – the satisfaction of knowing that they held any control over her. Deep down, Chō knew she was a strong, beautiful woman. Some innate part of her knew that if they would just take the time to truly see her, to look beyond their small bubble and stare deeper into this world they would marvel at her grandeur. Letting a bunch of strangers dictate her life was not her way. Chō would not bow down in the slightest.

VI

Slipping out of her jūnihitoe, Chō snuck a glance out of the corner of her eye to see if Shōtarō was looking. Her porcelain skin glowed in the soft light – her curves catching the shadows in just the right places to accentuate her figure. However, Shōtarō stood off to the side, inspecting his armor. A spike of anger flashed in her, but Chō quickly suppressed the emotion.

"What are you thinking about, otto?" Her words exuded seduction, but if he was paying attention Shōtarō would have also noticed the steel buried underneath. "I'm a little chilly. Won't you help warm me?"

For the first time, Shōtarō turned to face her with a sigh. Time out in the countryside hunting the rōnin did not treat him kindly. His face had become hard and gaunt. The unspoken horrors he must have seen out there left an imprint on his soul – his stoic mask unable to hide the haunting images.

Now completely exposed, Chō sauntered over to him. She swayed her hips with each step, a flirtatious smile on her lips. Wrapping her arms around Shōtarō's waist, Chō pressed herself against his bare chest. Her breasts gently rubbed against him as she held him tight. Her hips pressed on his manhood. Meeting his gaze, Chō chewed on her bottom lip once more. She could feel his body react to hers.

Men were so quick to forgive.

†

"Police have confirmed that there is no new information on last night's attack." The headline on a local newspaper stood out so bold that it was almost as though someone yelled into the little local convenience store. In smaller text, Chō read: "They believe it may be an isolated incident, but warn the public to remain cautious."

Unconsciously, Chō's hand went to the mask on her face. Her head no longer throbbed, but she remembered the faint memory she'd had earlier, more a hunch than any true memory, that she'd hit her head on her way into her apartment the previous night. The melonpan's wrapper crinkled as her hand reflexively clenched. Turning from the refrigerator, Chō abandoned the drinks she'd been contemplating.

The door of the konbini tinkled behind her as Chō wandered out onto the streets. The melonpan still clenched in her hand was forgotten as she moved in a daze. Deep within, the uncomfortable truth of a young child being killed moments after they met unnerved her. The thought that it could have been her killed instead of the child brought with it an unsettling vulnerability that Chō wanted to push away. It easily could have been her who fell prey to this monster.

No longer hungry, Chō tossed the unopened pastry into the nearest bin. The thump as it hit the bottom echoed in her empty world. She traveled in a void – a place where only she existed.

The sun hung low in the sky, but dusk was still hours away. She traveled during that waiting time where children were in their afternoon classes longing to go home. The unexpected appearance of a young boy broke the spell.

As he neared, Chō blinked heavily, bringing him into focus. He was a cute kid, the dimples by his mouth giving him a cherubic appearance.

"Why are you crying, Onee-chan?"

His words came out with the innocence only a toddler could bring. A lollipop dangled from his chubby hand, its bright colors waiting to be enjoyed. Emotion burst from Chō's chest like a dam. That overwhelming sense of vulnerability proved to be too much for her to handle. Tears spilled down her cheeks as the first moment of kindness that day touched her.

"Am I pretty?" she asked through gasps.

Embarrassment burned her cheeks. Thanking the face mask that hid her face, Chō cursed herself for baring her soul to such a young child. The need to feel special overcame her.

Bewildered, the little boy nodded in affirmation. Not for the first time in the last couple days, relief flooded Chō. She wanted to properly show her gratitude to him with a sincere smile and moved to take off her mask. As she removed the mask and shoved it in her bag, a wide smile plastered on her face at finally being seen, the little boy waved his lollipop in front of her. Chō took the gift, a little apprehensive from taking candy from a baby, but nonetheless pleased at the unexpected treat. The candy caught the light in an unusual way – the reds sparkling like rubies. By the time Chō finished examining the gift, the boy disappeared down the street.

†

Sitting on the cool linoleum floor, Chō spun the lollipop between her fingers. The waning light of the setting sun filtering through her window caught the bright colors, mesmerizing her with the depth of their sparkle. For a fleeting moment, she wondered if her soul sparkled just as dazzlingly.

It was strangely soothing. The simple, childish colors – red, yellow, blue, and pink – reminded Chō of a field of flowers. Almost like the ones she might see in a dream.

Feeling more at peace than she had in a while, Chō climbed onto a chair and drifted off to sleep.

VII

Chō's lips pressed lightly against Shōtarō's. The familiar warmth excited her. Though she had many lovers, Shōtarō remained her favorite, despite what she told Tatsuzō. Her long, shiny hair flowed down her back, hiding any marks her young lover or the others may have left.

Shōtarō hesitated before returning his wife's affection. A ravenous hunger filled Chō. She pressed her lips against his harder, letting her lust overcome her. His body tried to resist, but Chō knew it was futile. The two shared an energy that tied them together. Intense. Electrifying.

Shōtarō was hers.

†

The crackle of the television woke Chō with a start. Her body ached as she stretched in her tiny chair. Her neck hurt from the awkward angle she crammed it in before falling asleep last night. Stretching it from side-to-side to release the tension, she sat upright in her chair. The cool voice of the male news anchor came on, breaking the static.

"The recommended curfew has not been lifted," he said. "Despite no new evidence coming to light, due to the violent nature of the crime, police urge everyone to remain vigilant."

The reporter carried on in the background as Chō made her way to the kitchen.

"Like after school clubs would be closed," Chō groused. "Let them figure it out on their own."

Her discomfort left her grumpy. The cup of tea warming her hands couldn't even act as a balm.

A low growl escaped her lips as she dropped into her chair and turned off the television. Her nerves couldn't handle any more bad news. Sucking on the pop absentmindedly, Chō glowered at the dark television screen. The sugary confection didn't help soothe her nerves.

†

The heat welled within her as Chō wrapped her arms around her husband, pressing him closer. She wanted him. Craved him. As his hands slid between her legs, her body trembled. Chō waited for his touch. Soon, they would be a bundle of arms and legs.

Why was he taking so long?

"Do you take me for a fool?" Steel coated every syllable, but like a true warrior, Shōtarō maintained his composure.

He sat up, glaring at Chō. Confused, she moved to sit up, but he pushed her down roughly.

"Answer me."

His command rang in the room. The very power of his words kept Chō rooted on the ground as they reverberated in the air. The silence stretched. Before she could react, Shōtarō's hand shot out. The sound of the slap echoed hauntingly around them. He struck her with such force that her head snapped back. A dribble of blood ran from the corner of her mouth.

Instead of cowering, Chō fought back a giggle. She could feel the black hatred that she struggled to contain whenever he wasn't fulfilling her physical needs seeping into her. The loathing reflected her very soul despite the deranged grin that crept across her face.

"I needed something to occupy my time while you were away." Ice coated every venomous word. "What would you have me do?"

"Maybe respect my sacrifice and keep your damn legs closed."

Neither yelled. Yet the rage that engulfed the room swirled like a miasma around them.

"A beautiful woman like me should have her every desire fulfilled."

"At what cost? What if you carried his child?" The rage behind his words caused his voice to quiver.

"How do you know I'm not already?"

Placing her hand over her exposed belly, Chō flashed another smile. However, Shōtarō called her bluff.

VIII

Brilliant oranges mixed with deep purples and blues so dark they could be black filtered through the window. True pinks wove a river of light between the ever-deepening darkness of night as akane, the color of sunset, painted the world before black monochrome blanketed the earth. It painted a perfect picture of the endless waltz of time onto her floor. Bits of red, yellow, blue, and pink – the remnants of a shattered lollipop, lay strewn on the cool linoleum.

In the corner by her table, Chō sat on her pale pink cushion. The shadows wrapped around her, pulling her away from the beauty of akane's light. Her usually immaculate hair hung limp and stringy. The delicate make-up that enhanced her face was gone, wiped off the night before.

The metallic tang of blood filled her mouth as she gnawed on the inside of her cheek. She needed to stop, but found she couldn't.

A primal scream tore from Chō's throat as all the anguish she'd built up throughout the day finally broke free like water from a dam. It rang out loud and shrill. She only stopped when her voice became hoarse and the scream threatened to shred her throat.

†

"Sakanoue-sama!" The pleading cry of the serving girl sounded so far away. "Please Sakanoue-sama!"

Shōtarō didn't appear to listen to the entreaties. Chō realized she pushed him too far this time. With all of his suspicions confirmed, his pent-up anger could no longer be contained. Chō scurried backwards, her hands futilely attempting to shield her naked body. The fury that flashed in his eyes sent a wave of cold fear coursing through her. Shōtarō swatted away the young servant as she feebly tried to restrain him. The girl recoiled with a whimper.

"Otto," Chō found herself saying. "Please forgive me." She hated how her voice quivered.

Chō stopped as her back hit a wall and she could go no further. Shōtarō was on her in an instant. His fingers grabbed a handful of her hair and lifted her up. Tears welled in Chō's eyes as he yanked her closer to him.

"Please," she begged.

Her heart began to pound in her chest as his fury seemed to know no end.

"You live your life by your own desires," Shōtarō spat. The venom in his voice chilled Chō's soul. "Your vanity and need for attention has shamed my family for years. But not anymore."

Unsheathing a thin silver blade from the waist of his hakama, Shōtarō readjusted his grip until he squeezed Chō's face with his free hand. Chō's eyes widened as he pressed the blade to her lips. She tried to turn away, but Shōtarō was too strong. A pitiful whimper escaped Chō as he slipped the blade between her lips and inside her mouth. Her eyes and nose ran, leaving her normally flawless face dirty and slick.

"Please," she begged once more.

The words came out garbled and sounded like gibberish, her tongue unable to move with the blade in her mouth. Hearing herself sound like the uneducated peasants that lived in the nearby village brought tears of anger to Chō's eyes and her face burned. Her entreaties fell on deaf ears. Her knees gave out from under her, but Shōtarō didn't seem to notice. His eyes burned as he held her gaze – his anger unwavering.

Fear gripped Chō. Her head swam as she struggled to breathe, but it was as though someone clamped on her throat with an iron grip. Her heart pounded faster. Time stood still as the two stared into the depths of each other's souls. The kindness inside Shōtarō that Chō had fallen in love with disappeared, consumed by the flames of her betrayal. Gone was the sweet man who gently tucked a strand of her hair behind her ear before slipping a blossom just above it. No more did she see the man who sent her poems while he served the regent. The man before her now glared at her with eyes colder than tempered steel.

A moment later, a searing pain shot through her face, unblocking her throat so she could cry out as the blade slid through her flesh. First, one side of her mouth, then the other. Warm blood ran down the sides of Chō's face as she fell to the floor in a sobbing, crumpled heap.

Around her, all was silent.

†

Darkness embraced Chō like an old friend. She relished the nearly empty streets, letting the silence soothe her. Why should she let the oblivious assholes of the world dictate her mood? No more. She would not let the rudeness of strangers or the fear of a random attacker keep her from enjoying a crisp, serene evening like she had countless nights before.

She wished she could find some of that peace right now though.

The chilled night air blew through Chō's now-sleek hair. The cold felt nice on her face and dissipated the heat of her negativity. Her solitude let her tackle the many emotions that had been simmering inside her all day. As she had been doing for the last few days.

Her emotions tangled in her chest like a knotted mess of yarn. With each step, she worked through the tangle. Slowly, one section then another became free. Like the pieces of a puzzle, each bit of the yarn brought her thoughts and emotions into focus, helping Chō find herself once more. The loneliness she'd felt a few days ago faded, and she finally felt like she had a sense of direction. A smile spread on her lips under the face mask she had worn to hide her scowl.

The final string of yarn glowed in the yellow light of a nearby streetlamp next to the konbini. Inside, she noted a group of high school girls laughing and smiling. Tucking a strand of hair behind her ear, Chō set off with determined steps. She found herself yet again.

IX

Wandering through a busier side of town, Chō heard the tinkle of a konbini and was suddenly bathed in harsh, artificial light. A group of teenaged girls walked out with sandwiches in hand and laughing. Chō's stomach rumbled. It had been a while since she had gone out for a late-night snack.

"Are you seeing Yūta-kun later?" one of the girls asked.

Another girl hummed in response. Like Chō, she put a lot of effort into looking cute, embracing the hime gyaru aesthetic. Her hair was dyed a light brown and pulled into gently curled pigtails, tied up with trailing pink ribbons. "We're going out for karaoke tonight." Her voice came out highly-pitched and saccharine.

Was it not even nine? These girls should be in their cram school.

The thought filled Chō with loathing. She felt like an old woman.

The other girls squealed in excitement, causing Ribbon to grin proudly. They congratulated her, begging Ribbon to tell them all about her date later that night. Looking both shy yet pleased, Ribbon's perfect porcelain cheeks became the softest shade of pink – nearly matching the color of her ribbons. The girls disappeared down the street, a trail of giggling and animated chatter trailing behind them.

Chō's jaw clenched and she felt a tug of rage as the yarn she worked so hard to untangle within pulled free one-by-one. Gritting her teeth, Chō set off behind them. With each thread Chō pulled free, she found herself gaining clarity over the previous days' frustrations.

X

Chō's body quaked, her breath coming in uneven gasps. Warm blood trickled down her face tracing a path to her collarbone before pooling onto her chest and dribbling down further. Trembling, she reached up to touch her mangled face slick with her lifeblood. The blood mixed with tears, turning her normally pristine exterior into something unrecognizable.

Shōtarō towered over her, glowering at the mess. He took no pleasure in his actions; Chō could see it on his face. Shōtarō had always been a pragmatic man, one who took the time to think out the consequences of his actions. Sometimes Chō wished he followed his desires, more like her. This all could have been avoided if he did.

"What have you done to me?" Chō spat, flecks of blood flying with each word.

Her wounds made her mouth feel floppy and her words come out slurred as though she'd had too much to drink. Chō felt her cheeks burn as color rushed to her face. The way the words tumbled out of her mouth like a lazy drunkard shamed her. Years of practicing the royal dialect as a child all gone to waste.

Her hand went to her mutilated face in an effort to stop the bleeding once more. The shock wore off, but her body continued to tremble. Chō usually maintained her composure, but her husband's betrayal – how he ruined her beautiful face – pushed her rage to the surface, stoking the fires until they boiled over. Chō's rich, brown eyes turned black, mirroring the hatred in her heart. She wanted him to feel her wrath.

"I've made it so your outside now reflects what's within," Shōtarō replied calmly.

"But my face!" she sputtered.

In the background, the young house servant muttered quietly, incoherently as her back hugged the wall. The poor girl's eyes wide in terror, locked on Chō and her bloody mess. Chō would deal with the girl later.

"Your mask has fallen off. You are exposed."

Chō's fingers curled into trembling fists as she struggled to push herself up from the floor. Blood dropped from her face, the drips pattering against the tiles. Her foot slipped beneath her, dropping Chō to her knee. Using the wall for leverage, Chō managed to regain her footing. Each step threatened to send her skidding in her own slippery blood, but she didn't care. Chō's focus remained on her husband.

She no longer bothered to cradle the wounds on her face. The worst of the bleeding had slowed. Behind her, smeared handprints painted the wall – thin red streaks where she'd clawed her way upright, dragging herself from the cold ground.

Chō's breath came out in ragged gasps. Both pain and a blinding rage forced her to struggle to breathe, but Chō didn't notice. All she saw was red.

†

Calls of good-bye echoed in the calm night. Each farewell became quieter as the group of girls split off one-by-one until only Ribbon remained. It must be getting closer to nine. The girl checked her phone before taking off. Not wanting to follow her much longer, Chō did not pause; instead, she picked up her pace to close the distance between them.

†

Pain blossomed in Chō's chest. Her breath caught in her throat, a soft moan breaking free. Warm blood dribbled from the katana blade embedded in her flesh. She stared down at the blade then back up to her husband, her body trembling in shock once more. Her mouth hung agape, eyes wide, struggling to comprehend what she was seeing.

"How?" she stammered. Chō attempted to repeat the question, but her words couldn't break free from her mouth.

Shōtarō stared down at her, expressionless.

"Sh- Shō…" The words died on Chō's lips.

A gasp escaped Chō as Shōtarō pulled his blade free from her body, wiping it on his hakama before sheathing it. The blade now gone, Chō's wound began to bleed freely. Blood ran between her breasts and down her front. The dark red stood out on her porcelain skin. Streaks from where she'd rubbed her dirty hands earlier further marred her perfect flesh.

Shōtarō kept her gaze. Something about how he maintained eye contact with her, unwavering, unnerved her. Tears no longer poured from her eyes. Her heart no longer raced. Chō was alone. Empty. She looked to the house servant for any sign of emotion. The young girl stood pressed against the wall, hugging herself as she gaped at Chō. Tears rained from the young girl's wide eyes.

Seeing the girl tremble as she huddled against the wall brought a small smile to Chō's face. However, her strength quickly faded as blackness raced to greet her. Throughout it all, Shōtarō watched her.

As he faded into the darkness, Chō smiled.

She was at peace.

†

Chō walked in step with Ribbon, just a few paces behind her, but had had enough. She cleared her throat and Ribbon spun around, nonplussed as she finished sending off a text.

"I'm sorry," Ribbon said distractedly as she scooted over for Chō to pass.

The light from Ribbon's phone shone in the dark. Chō vaguely wondered if her sweetheart had sent her a message. Not continuing further, Chō stopped in front of the girl. Ribbon watched Chō with cautious eyes. Chō could see confusion and distrust fighting for dominance. The mixture of competing emotions brought a smile to Chō's lips. The uncertainty helped her own swirling emotions become calm.

"Am I pretty?"

No preamble. Chō didn't have time for pleasantries. A flicker of confusion passed over Ribbon's face. Chō felt a twinge of annoyance. Her hand twitched, reaching for her cherry blossom hairpin. The moment passed as Ribbon plastered on a pleasant smile and nodded.

"Of course." Ribbon's voice carried an undertone of concern that hadn't gone away.

Chō gnashed her teeth. Her beauty shouldn't be a question. Ripping off her mask and removing the hairpin to let her onyx hair fall freely around her, Chō took a step forward and held Ribbon's gaze.

"What about now?"

A wide grin spread over Chō's face. The disrespect she'd been feeling the last few days proved to be too much. She was ready to punish the next person who dared upset her.

Ribbon's eyes went wide and she took a step back. Her smile faltered, but didn't disappear. Her hand shook as she held up her phone for Chō to see. Like a mirror, Chō looked back at herself in the phone's camera. The bloody scars at the corner of her mouth, seemed preternaturally bright, giving her a perpetual nightmarish grin. The shadows from a nearby streetlamp cast dark shadows under her eyes and accentuated the gruesome disfigurement on her face. She looked otherworldly.

A wave of emotion rushed over her as the feeling of being lost and isolated vanished. Memories of the man who ruined her flashed before her eyes. This was his fault, that damn Shōtarō. The final bit of yarn was pulled free and her hairpin clattered to the ground, forgotten.

†

The ceremony was a quiet affair. Shōtarō and the house staff lit incense and said a prayer in front of Chō's picture. None of her lovers bothered to bring flowers. Not that Shōtarō would have allowed it. The young serving girl stood next to Shōtarō, his arm resting around her shoulder. The girl had never been the same since that night. Watching her husband act so familiar to someone of such low social status made her blood boil.

"Good-bye, Milady," Chō heard the girl whisper.

Anger flared within her. The house girl, someone with no social standing, was the only one to say good-bye. Spinning on her heel, Chō stormed out of her house and disappeared into the night.

XI

Ribbon was long gone. Her phone proved to be a good distraction for Chō. By the time she returned from her reverie, Ribbon had run away and the streets had become relatively quiet. Slipping her face mask on once more, Chō took to wandering the streets.

She moved easily between the few people who still traversed them at night. Her mind, however, was both lost and clear as the pieces of yarn were finally separated. Centuries of wandering the mortal realm had erased her memories. But now, seeing her face in Ribbon's camera brought them back. Chō remembered who she was.

She was yōkai.

‡‡‡

About the Author

K.N. Nguyen is a fantasy author and founder of DragonScript. Growing up, she often found herself immersed in some imaginary world, conquering enemy nations, and saving the day. As time went on, her love for horrible puns and nerd culture pulled her out of these worlds and brought her back to reality.

It wasn't until she started working at her office job that she felt the itch to begin writing. Since 2015, she's been bringing her stories to life, one-by-one, and following her passion by delving into new mythologies.

A native of Sacramento, California, K.N. Nguyen spends her time singing karaoke, playing taiko, enjoying rhythm dancing games, and traveling with her friends and family when she isn't writing.

Also by K.N. Nguyen

The Fallen Series

King's Blood

Oath Blood

God's Blood

Nightmare Blood

Dragon Script

Dragon Script

Lost Chapter

Other Works

A Song of Strength

Last Chance

www.ingramcontent.com/pod-product-compliance
Lightning Source LLC
Chambersburg PA
CBHW071952190726
48293CB00004B/1439